For Milou, my little godson whom I adore . . . and
a philosophical nod to his Papi Babu!
V. M.

Leo, Nina — my loves — may your lives be as close to your dreams as possible!
P. N.

© for the original French edition: L´Élan vert, Saint-Pierre-des-Corps, 2016
© for the English edition: Prestel Verlag, Munich • London • New York, 2017

Prestel Verlag, Munich · London · New York
A member of Verlagsgruppe Random House GmbH
www.prestel.com

English translation: Agathe Joly

Copy-editing: Brad Finger
Project management: Mareike Rinke
Typesetting: textum GmbH
Production management: Lisa Preissler

Printing and binding: TBB, a. s.
Paper: Condat matt Périgord

Printed in Slovakia

ISBN 978-3-7913-7279-2

A Children's Book
Inspired by
Wassily Kandinsky

THE DREAMING GIANT

VÉRONIQUE MASSENOT

PEGGY NILLE

Prestel
Munich · London · New York

There once was a tiny little world
where skyscrapers, cities, and highways
were no taller than a few feet.
And the people of this world, the Krobz,
measured less than an inch.

But one day,
out of the blue,
without any real explanation,
a GIANT
stepped into their world.

WHAT A PANIC!

With his shoes size 612, you could say
he had put his huge foot in it! What did he want?
Was he just a peaceful neighbor coming to them for a friendly visit?
Was he the scout of a hostile people about to invade them?
While the Giant was taking a picnic break,
the left side of his bottom squashing the zoo
and the right side mashing the botanical gardens,
the Krobz began to ponder.

After he had eaten his super-sized sandwich, the Giant became full and fell asleep.
Quick, it's time to take action: we have to understand what he wants!
A trio of courageous Krobz — Zig, Zag, and the young Swirl —
volunteered to take part in an exploration.
"Follow me!" ordered Zig, the more experienced one. "All we have to do is enter
through the mouth and let ourselves glide through the deep pipe.
You'll see, it will be just like going down a slide."

The first Krobz disappeared through the opening,

closely followed by his fellow adventurers.

"How beautiful!," said Zag.

Inside, the light was softly colored in pink …
and a funny little bubble floated before them.

"Cells!," said Zig. "Let's step aboard them
and see where they take us.
They'll work perfectly as travelling machines!"

Unfortunately, they soon hit a traffic jam, and Swirl began to grow impatient.

"Move ahead, you silly cells! Come on … faster, let's circulate!"

All of a sudden, Zag shouted "HURRAY!"

She had just made radio contact with Krobz headquarters,

thanks to her telepathic antenna.

"Hello, hello!," the three explorers called out.

"Can you hear me?"

"Yes, loud and clear! Where are you?

Give us your position!"

Zig, almost running into a group of speeding molecules, answered:

"According to the noise of our engine, we are approaching the heart!

How about on your side, nothing to report?"

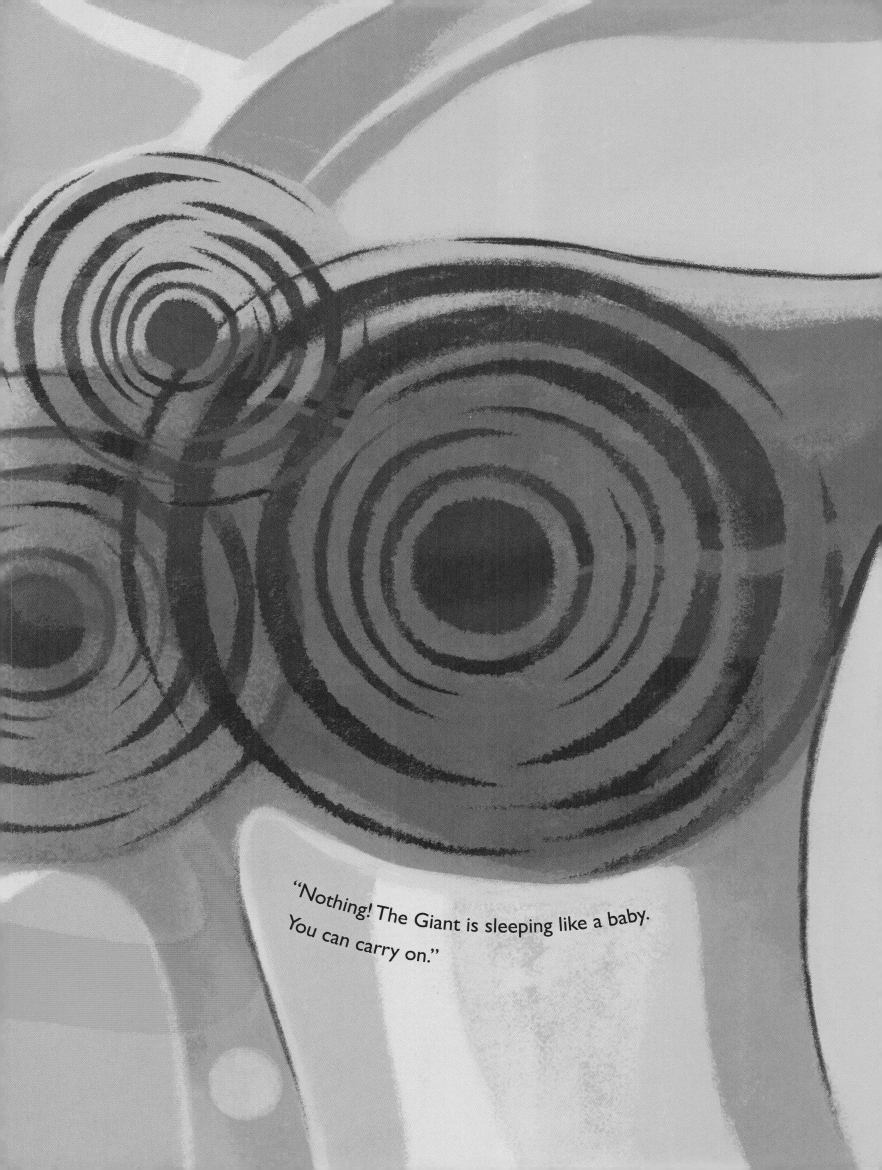

"Nothing! The Giant is sleeping like a baby. You can carry on."

Eventually, they arrived in the heart, where life was beating like a drum ...

Waves, red and blue, carried them through,

as the tempo lifted them up

making them want to dance, to go into a trance.

WHAT AN ATMOSPHERE!

As they were about to enter the heart's left ventricle,
young Swirl suddenly jumped off the vehicle.

"Listen up! I love this music.
It's like a chorus singing with a thousand voices!
It's marvelous! Let me stay here!"

But Zig wouldn't hear it.

He started the engine, caught up with the runaway, and made a turn into an artery.

"We're going against the tide: hold on guys and keep it cool! I can see the brain from here."

Swirl sighed:

"But earlier, in the heart, didn't you feel like you were part of something big? Wasn't it something even bigger than the Giant himself?"

"Shush!," answered Zig and Zag. "We're approaching the ear!"

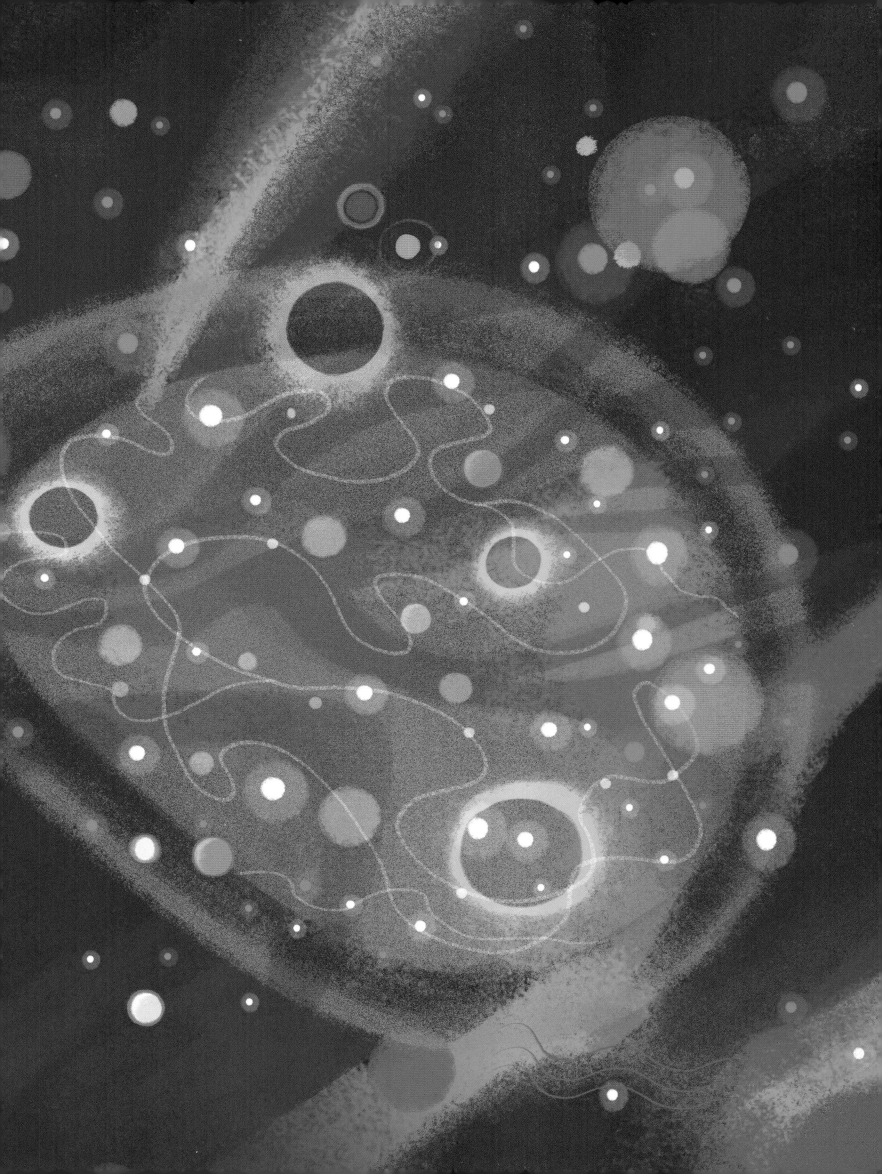

After parking their cell,
they entered the vestibule,
took the spiral staircase,
and finally discovered the command room.
For now, everything appeared to be on standby.
Only a few light switches
seemed to be blinking in the dark.
Zig looked at the control board.
"This is where exterior data comes in:
sound, smells, shapes, colors …
Look at this! The Giant apparently liked the taste
of his sandwich, but his buttocks seemed
to find the ground a little too hard!"

Alas, the explorers searched everywhere and found no sign of any reasons, either good or bad, for why the sleeping Giant had visited them.

Zig contacted the Krobz on the outside.

"Hello, hello? We haven't found anything conclusive ... Is he still deep asleep?"

"Well, no, actually! I was just about to call you!

His eyes are closed, but he flinched, turned around,

and scratched himself — giving us such a fright!

But he still hasn't woken up. Now he's smiling …

We think he might be dreaming.

Be careful!"

At that very instant in the command room, a window opened up.

Zig, Zag, and Swirl, blinded at first by the flow of light, slowly gathered around it.

What a show!

In a pure blue sky, dozens of kites were floating,

one more beautiful, colorful, and fun than the next.

Were they, perhaps, … alive?

One of the kites then came up to them.
"Hello little ones, would you like to go for a spin?"
The trio only hesitated a second before coming on board
for an extraordinary looping ride.

They felt so happy, so light, and so at peace in this airy setting.
They were surprised and overwhelmed
by all these shapes and colors …

There is no doubt that this strange creature
was an artist, and a great one at that.

There is nothing to fear from someone
who lives and thinks so beautifully and whose dreams are so GIGANTIC!

SKY BLUE

1940, oil on canvas, 100 x 73 cm,
Musée National d'Art Moderne, Paris, France

WASSILY KANDINSKY

Who was WASSILY KANDINSKY?

He was one of the most important artists of the 20th century because he "invented" abstract art, a type of painting that does not represent reality. Born in Moscow, Russia, in 1866, into a wealthy and cultured Jewish family, he decided to end his career as a teacher of law and economics and dedicate himself to art. Kandinsky admired the Impressionists, who used pure color to capture the effects of light in nature; and many of his first paintings were made in the Impressionist style. However, during a trip to Paris in 1906–7, he discovered artists who were exploring new and different ways of making art: Paul Cézanne, Henri Matisse, Pablo Picasso. Kandinsky soon decided to create his own modern style of art. In 1911, he and German painter Franz Marc founded the Blaue Reiter (or Blue Rider), a group of artists who abandoned realistic-looking pictures in favor of simple forms and bright, expressive colors. It was as a member of the Blaue Reiter that Kandinsky created his first great works of abstract art. Wassily later settled in Germany with Nina Andreevskaya, whom he married in 1917. He taught from 1922 to 1933 at the Bauhaus in Weimar — a famous school that developed a new vision of art, architecture, and design. In the 1930s, however, the German National Socialist government (the Nazis) took away Kandinsky's German nationality, which it also did for other Jews living in Germany. Wassily became stateless and moved to Paris, eventually becoming a French citizen in 1939. He died in the suburbs of Paris on December 13, 1944. His wife Nina died in 1980, 36 years after the artist, whose work she would promote for the rest of her life. Thanks to her determination and efforts, many of Kandinsky's paintings can now be admired in museums around the world. *Sky Blue*, for example, can be seen at the Centre George Pompidou in Paris.

WASSILY KANDINSKY

What is ABSTRACT ART?

Abstract art does not concern itself with depicting real-life figures, objects, and landscapes. Painting, instead, becomes a combination of shapes, lines, and colors that stands for itself, outside of anything in the natural world. Patches of color float freely across the canvas, while black lines create a kind of rhythm. For Kandinsky, these colors and images are like the melodies of musical instruments … melodies that generate emotions in the viewer.

GIANTS don't exist!

Why not? The Giant is a little like Kandinsky. He has the dreams of an artist: colored dreams! And when we enter his body, we discover a pink abstract universe and then a blue one with floating patches of color all around it. In a way, in this book, we witness the evolution of Kandinsky's work, from reality to abstraction.

What does SKY BLUE represent?

Nothing … and that's the point! Kandinsky made art that wasn't supposed to represent anything. Painted at the end of his life, this work is made in oil on a large canvas (39.4 x 28.7 inches, or 100 x 73 cm). Only one color is used, the color blue, in order to depict the start of a world with new poetic shapes and strange multicolored dreams that float lightly into space: an image representing the freedom of dreams.